Such a Little Mouse

By Alice Schertle

Illustrated by Stephanie Yue

SCHOLASTIC INC.

Way out in the wide world
there is a meadow.

In the middle of the meadow,
under a clump of dandelions,
there is a hole.

And way down deep in the hole lives a mouse.

Such a little mouse,

with his smart gray coat,

with his ears pink as petals,

with three twitchety whiskers on each side of his nose.

Every morning in spring,

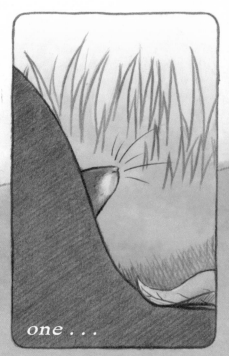

one . . .

two . . .

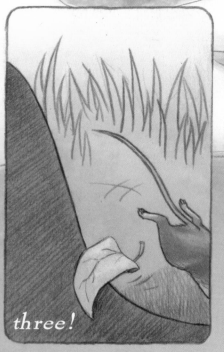

three!

He pops out of his hole.

Such a little mouse.
Off he goes into the wide world.

He sees a snail
climbing up a fern.

He watches the busy bees
on the clover blossoms.

"*Busy, busy, bizzzzzz,*"
say the bees.

He hears a woodpecker,
ratta-tat-tat-tat,
hammering a tree.

The little mouse looks
at himself in a puddle.
"Hello, self."

When the day is done,
he brings a little round seed
home in his mouth.

He packs it away in his storeroom,
way down deep in his hole.

Every morning in summer,

one . . .

two . . .

three!

He pops out of his hole.

Such a little mouse.
Off he goes into the wide world.

He watches the beavers working in the pond.

He visits a toad
who lives under a flowerpot.

"It's dark in here,"
says the little mouse.

"That's the way I like it,"
says the toad.

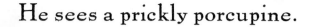
He sees a prickly porcupine.

When the day is done,
he brings a sprig of watercress
home in his mouth.

He packs it away in his storeroom,
way down deep in his hole.

Every morning in autumn,

one . . .

two . . .

three!

He pops out of his hole.

Such a little mouse.
Off he goes into the wide world.

He tunnels under piles of leaves.
Rustle, rustle, rustle, go the leaves.

He feels the autumn wind tickle his whiskers.
"Winter is coming," whispers the wind.

He watches the geese flying overhead.
"Honk! Honk!" they cry. "Winter is coming!"

He sees a line of tiny ants marching along.
The little mouse puts his petal-pink ear
close to the ground.

"Winter is coming!"
say the tiny ant voices.

When the day is done,
he carries an acorn home in his mouth.
He packs it away in his storeroom
way down deep in his hole.

One morning,
when the little mouse
pops out of his hole,
it is winter.

The grass and the flowers and the weeds are gone.

Snow covers the meadow and the trees.
"Brrrrrrr," says the little mouse.

Back he goes, down
into his warm hole.

He makes a loaf of acorn bread.

He makes seed-and-watercress soup.

He snuggles up under
a little moss blanket
with a book of mouse tales.

Such a little mouse,
all snug and warm,
deep down in his hole,
until spring.

For Jen and Drew, Kate and John,
Spence and Dylan, with such a lot of love — A.S.

For Chicken Legs, Paint Paws,
Heifer, Bainbridge, and The Stripeytails — S.Y.

ISBN 978-1-338-07855-8

12 11 10 9 8 7 6 5 4 3 2   17 18 19 20 21

Printed in the U.S.A.   40

First Scholastic paperback printing, April 2016

The text type was set in Pabst.
Book design by David Saylor and Charles Kreloff